Zippy's Big Difference

"Zippy's Big Difference is an excellent tool for parents and Christian therapists to enable children with physical deformities to work through their issues with God and eventually embrace their differences and see themselves as windows to Him."

Dr. Rick Metrick, LPC, ALPS
Director of Total Life Counseling, Inc.

"Zippy's Big Difference is well written and will hopefully open a lot of doors for discussions between adults and children about some of the tough faith-based questions that people face. It celebrates finding comfort with who you are and shows that we are all uniquely created."

Tony Memmel
Amputee and musician
www.TonyMemmel.com

"Celebrating differences is key to the way my husband and I are raising our daughter and sharing our experiences on my website. I am so happy to see a story that helps her to know she isn't alone with a limb difference."

Jen Lee Reeves
Blogger and advocate
Born Just Right (bornjustright.com)

Zippy's Big Difference

Written by Candida Sullivan

Illustrated by Jack Foster

Special note from Dr. Rick Metrick

Copyright @ 2012 ShadeTree Publishing, LLC

1038 N. Eisenhower Dr. #274

Beckley, West Virginia 25801

Print ISBN: 978-1-937331-31-3

e-Book ISBN: 978-1-937331-32-0

Visit our Web site at www.ShadeTreePublishing.com

To all of God's children. May you find and always celebrate your differences. C.S.

For my beautiful granddaughter, Keira, whose smile launches my heart.
Reach for the stars. Follow your dreams. Believe in today. Hope in tomorrow. Love always.
Even the smallest dream, with faith, hope, and love, can make the biggest difference. J.F.

"Even every one that is called by name:
for I have created him for my glory,
I have formed him; yea, I have made him."
                                    ISAIAH 43:7 KJV

This is a story about a zebra named Zippy who was different...

"Is it possible to cancel a prayer?" Zippy wondered.

He was in trouble—big, super-duper kind of trouble.

He tried to remember the prayer that changed everything. He cringed as he recalled it.

But somehow, his prayer had gotten all messed up. Zippy didn't mean for all of the clouds to fall from the sky. Surely, his mom would understand. He really didn't think she would, though.

"Oh God! I think You've misunderstood me. I didn't want You to make the clouds fall onto the ground. When my mom finds out, I will be in so much trouble. Cancel my prayer God. I take it all back," Zippy confessed.

Zippy felt relieved. He knew God would fix it all. But when he glanced outside, nothing had changed.

"Oh, this is bad. Really, really bad," Zippy stammered. "I will be grounded forever and ever and maybe longer," he imagined aloud.

Zippy raced outside and tried to think of a plan.

He had to get the clouds back in the sky. Immediately!
He rolled up one of the clouds and hurled it toward
the sky. Thump! It landed in his face. He wiped the
cold, wet cloud away and hurried to find his friends.

Zippy's friends were rolling around in the clouds, laughing and playing. Zippy explained his dilemma and begged them to help him. Golly pondered Zippy's request and shoved a huge cloud into his mouth. "These are delicious," he stated.

"Don't eat them!" Zippy yelled. "They have to go back in the sky."

Just then the other zebras shoved clouds into their mouth, too.

They were ignoring Zippy and eating the clouds. Zippy flopped down on a log and sighed.

"What am I going to do?" he asked.

"What's wrong, Zippy?" Naomi asked, from a tree branch.

Zippy explained it all to her.

"Oh, Zippy! You didn't make the clouds fall to the ground. That's snow," Naomi explained.

"So, I didn't do anything wrong?" Zippy asked. "Then what about my prayer?"

"Well, that was a selfish prayer, Zippy. You wanted it to stop raining because it would make you happy. You didn't think about the animals, trees, and plants that need the rain," Naomi explained.

Zippy dropped his head and nodded.

"Prayer is very special, and we need to make sure our heart is right when we do it," Naomi stated.

"How can I make sure my heart is right for the prayer?" Zippy asked.

"First of all, God is the One who gives our heart the desire to pray. So listen to your heart Zippy." Naomi continued, "And sometimes He gives more than one person the same prayer to pray. In the Bible, God tells us that when two or more come together in prayer that He will hear it.

Just then Golly and his friends approached. "That's wonderful news, Zippy!" Golly declared. "We can all pray for God to give you black stripes. Then, you will never be teased or stared at for looking different."

Zippy smiled. Golly's plan sounded wonderful.

"Will that work? Will God hear our prayers?" Zippy asked with new excitement.

"I don't know, Zippy," said Naomi. "What if God has a great purpose for giving you all white stripes? What if He has a beautiful plan for your life? God doesn't make mistakes. So, your stripes have a reason. It wasn't an accident that you received all white stripes," she explained.

"If it's so great then why does everyone stare at me? Why do they tease me and laugh? Why do they always ask what happened to me?" Zippy asked.

"Maybe you are their window to God. When they see you it reminds them miracles are real, and anything is possible with God," Naomi explained.

"But, how?" Zippy questioned.

"When you helped your friends escape the hyenas and crocodiles, you showed incredible courage. You showed everyone it was possible to be brave, despite the width of your stripes. You gave the zebras hope," Naomi answered.

"Really?" Zippy asked.

Naomi nodded.

Zippy watched as Golly whispered to the zebras, and they whispered to the crocodiles. The crocodiles whispered to the birds, and they called to the others—even the hyenas.

In unison, all of the animals in Grassy Plains bowed their head to pray.

Zippy knew it was possible for God to fix his stripes. He knew God could do it in a moment. With time seeming to stand still—everyone waited for his response.

For a moment, Zippy wanted those black stripes. He wanted to be normal just like everyone else. But then he also wanted all of the beautiful things that God had planned, <u>just for him</u>.

Zippy didn't know what to do. He thought about all of the nights he had cried. He thought about the bullies who teased him. And then, he remembered about all of the animals he had helped.

"Stop!" Zippy yelled.

"Why?" Golly asked. "We're about to help you get black stripes."

"I don't want black stripes," Zippy confessed. "God gave me all white stripes for a reason. He made me exactly like He wanted me to be. And I don't want to change them. I like being different."

All of the animals stared at Zippy in amazement. They pondered his statement.

Just then, Golly declared, "I'm different, too. See, my left ear is a little longer than my right one."

"Well, I'm bigger than all the other crocodiles, and my teeth are crooked," Mr. Crocodile piped up.

"What about me?" one of the hyenas asked. "I'm purple. Have you ever seen a purple hyena before?"

"Don't forget me!" another hyena exclaimed. "I'm pink—And I'm a boy!"

And so it went in the land of Grassy Plains that everyone found their difference.

But Zippy thought his difference was the best of all because...

he could hide in the snow better than anyone else.

The End

A NOTE FROM DR. RICK METRICK

Zippy's Big Difference takes the reader beyond the emotional struggles facing children with physical disabilities and tackles some of the tough spiritual issues: Why did God allow me to be this way? Why doesn't He heal me? Doesn't God want me to be happy? Candida Sullivan's second book in Zippy's adventures is challenging, heart-warming, and real-to-life.

Parents and Christian therapists are encouraged to use Zippy's struggles with God's purpose as a springboard to help physically deformed children face, accept, and overcome their individual struggles with God.

Discussion Suggestions:

- For most of us, happiness is a high priority. What prevents you from being happy? What do you think it would take to make you happy? Do you know people who have what you want? Are they happy? Is anything more important than being happy?

- Zippy's story begins with Isaiah 43:7 – "Even every one that is called by my name: for I have created him for my glory, I have formed him; yea, I have made him" (KJV). In this verse, we discover why we were created. Does Isaiah 43:7 change your answer to "Is anything more important than being happy?"

- Naomi told Zippy that he had prayed "a selfish prayer." Is it alright to ask God for something you really want? When Jesus asked God for something He really wanted, He revealed that there was something He desired even more (see Matthew 26:39, 42). What do you desire most, your wants or God's wants?

- Zippy's friends felt sorry for him and, out of love, they wanted to ask God to take away his difference. Sometimes God answers prayers for healing, but many times He does not. Can you think of any reason God would not heal your concern? One reason is found in John 9:3 and another in 2 Corinthians 12:9.

- Naomi said, "What if God has a great purpose for giving you all white stripes? What if He has a beautiful plan for your life? God doesn't make mistakes. So, your stripes have a reason." Even more important to the human spirit than happiness is purpose. We can endure much if we know that there is a divine purpose for our difficulties. This should allow for discussion on how your child's difference is actually a gift from God to glorify Him and to reach others.

- Zippy struggled with not being like everyone else. He had been teased and bullied many times, just because he was different. But, when he realized that having no black stripes was God's perfect plan for his life he cried out, "I don't want to change them. I like being different." Why did Zippy like being different? Is there anything you like about being different?

- To Zippy's surprise, all of his friends were different in some way. This discovery allows for discussion concerning the many ways people are different. Everyone has a unique difference that he or she must learn to accept and embrace as God's will.

 Dr. Rick Metrick has a PhD in Christian Counseling Psychology and is a Licensed Professional Counselor (LPC) and Approved Licensed Professional Supervisor (ALPS). He is the senior pastor of Jones Memorial Baptist Church and the Director of Total Life Counseling located in Beckley, West Virginia. Rick is also the founder of the Just Honor God Foundation (www.JustHonorGod.com), host of God's Wake-Up Call Podcast, and author of several books including *Just Honor God: The 27-Day Challenge* and *God's Wake-Up Call*.

ABOUT THE AUTHOR

Candida Sullivan believes in miracles. She was born with a rare condition called Amniotic Band Syndrome, which generally causes death in most babies before they are ever born. She knows that it a beautiful blessing she survived and wants to show the world that her scars are not a punishment, but instead are a wonderful expression exemplifying God's love and mercy for her life. She believes God spared her for a reason and wants to spend her life telling of the hope and love God placed inside of her.

She also believes in dreams and knows God can make them come true. When her first book, *Zippy and the Stripes of Courage*, was published, Candida had no idea it would become a best seller as well as a finalist for a Reader's Favorite Award. She knows God makes the reality even better than the dreams.

Candida lives in Tennessee with her husband Shannon and two boys, Cayden and Jordon. She teaches Sunday school and loves to be surrounded by the wonder and excitement of kids.

See Zippy in his first book titled *Zippy and the Stripes of Courage*.

See also Candida's book for adults, *Underneath the Scars*, for her story about how she overcame her struggles of dealing with Amniotic Band Syndrome.

ABOUT THE ILLUSTRATOR

Jack Foster was born in Chicago Illinois and attended the American Academy of Art in Chicago. After several years as political cartoonist for the Elgin Courier News, Jack knew that he wanted to take his God-given talent in a different direction. While teaching Sunday school in 2006, he made the decision to pursue children's book illustrating. God has blessed him with the opportunity to illustrate over a dozen books. He is married, with five children and ten grandchildren.

ABOUT AMNIOTIC BAND SYNDROME

Amniotic Band Syndrome (ABS) is a rare condition caused by string-like bands in the amniotic sac. These bands can entangle the umbilical cord or other parts of the baby's body. The constriction can cause a variety of problems depending on where they are located and how tightly they are wrapped. The complications from ABS vary. Mild banding can result in amputation or scarring, while severe banding can result in death of the baby.

The medical community cannot truly explain what causes amniotic bands to form. While some call it a fluke of nature, I believe it is a symbol of God's amazing miracles. God doesn't punish us with scars; He blesses us with life. The scars show the world that there is a God and He is great.

AUTHOR'S ACKNOWLEDGEMENTS

I would like to thank God, foremost—the center of my life. My God exemplifies everything wonderful, beautiful, great, and loving in my life. Thank you God, for allowing Zippy to have another story and for all of the hearts it touched, for allowing me to visit schools, and for all of the lives you blessed us to touch. And most of all, thank you for loving me and allowing me to live, for giving me scars to remind me of your great love and mercy just for me and my life.

Thank you to everyone who read *Zippy and the Stripes of Courage* and loved Zippy so much that you asked for another story. To all of the schools, classrooms, homes, and hearts who welcomed us so greatly; who reads Zippy over and over to your children; who shared their stories of struggle and triumph with me; who supported Zippy and made him so successful. Your prayers, kindness, love and support mean so much to me.

Thank you to ShadeTree Publishing for making every part of this journey so wonderful! For caring about me as well as my cause and for working so hard to make it all happen. I'm so thankful God sent me you to help me along my journey.

Thank you to Jack Foster, my illustrator and friend, for giving me extra beautiful illustrations and for bringing Zippy's story to life. Thank you to Rick Metrick for sharing your knowledge and expertise and support.

Last, but not least my family. I couldn't do any of this without you! It's because of your love, prayers, and all of the special things you do to help me that I'm able to live my dreams.

See Zippy in his first book:

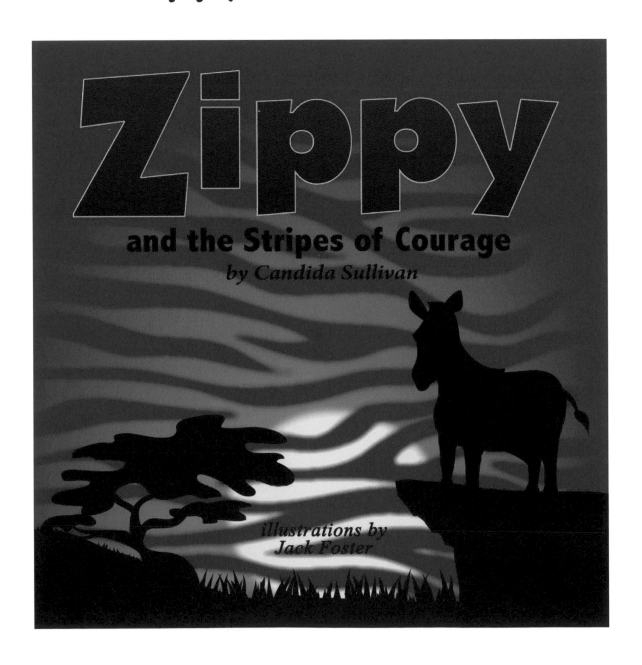

Zippy
and the Stripes of Courage
by Candida Sullivan

illustrations by
Jack Foster

CPSIA information can be obtained
at www.ICGtesting.com
Printed in the USA
LVIC06n0758060614
388666LV00009B/69

* 9 7 8 1 9 3 7 3 3 1 3 1 3 *